Sweet Tooth Bun

by Michael Scotto
illustrated by The Ink Circle

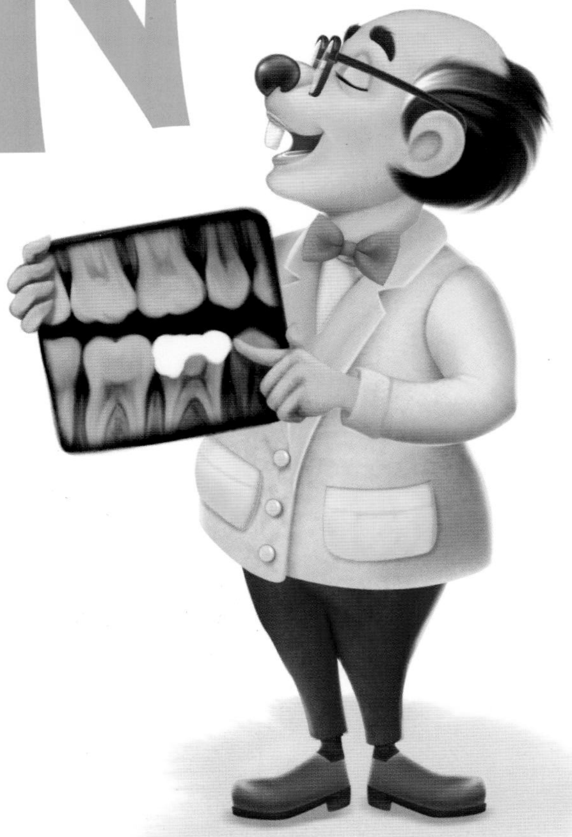

Welcome
to Midlandia
our Story Begins

Midlandia University
Playland Park
Town Square
Animal Land
HERE
Harvest Farms
Bike Factory

Starring
Bun O. BoBo
The Baker
Dr. Brushy
Wannadogood
The Dentist

Bun the baker
was famous for his sweets. Cakes and pies, cream puffs and cookies—Bun baked them all. If a treat looked less than perfect, Bun would not serve it. He would just eat it himself.

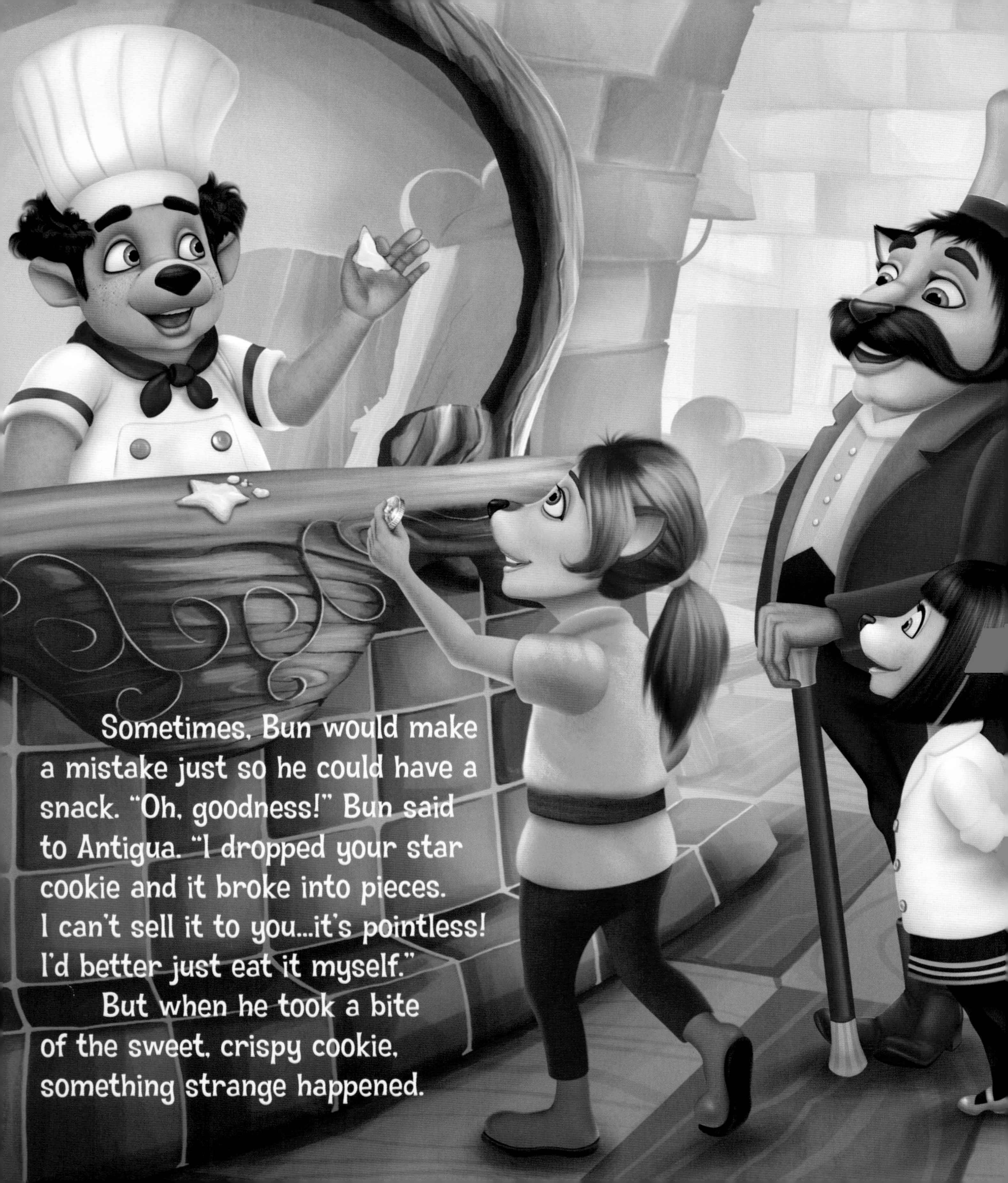

Sometimes, Bun would make a mistake just so he could have a snack. "Oh, goodness!" Bun said to Antigua. "I dropped your star cookie and it broke into pieces. I can't sell it to you...it's pointless! I'd better just eat it myself."

But when he took a bite of the sweet, crispy cookie, something strange happened.

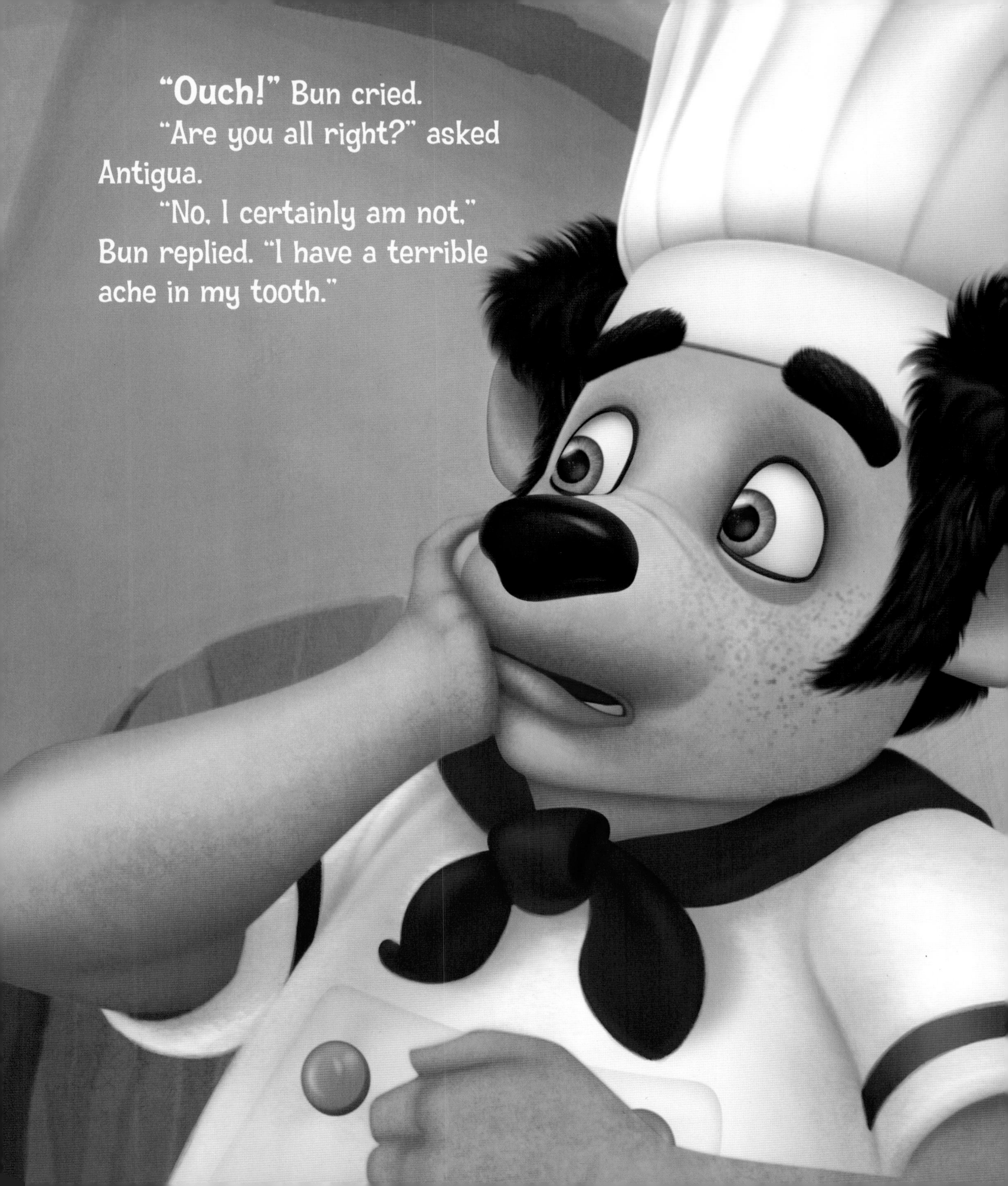

"Ouch!" Bun cried.

"Are you all right?" asked Antigua.

"No, I certainly am not," Bun replied. "I have a terrible ache in my tooth."

"A toothache? That's the worst!" Antigua said. "Maybe you should pay a visit to Dr. Brushy."

Bun turned whiter than whipped cream. "You mean...go to the dentist?" he asked.

"When your teeth hurt," Antigua said, "the dentist is the one to see."

"No, no," Bun said. "Remember when I said my toothache was terrible? I was only kidding then. See?" He took another nibble, wincing with each crunch. **"Oww, oww...I mean, yum-yum!"**

Antigua would not be fooled. "Come on, Bun," she said. "I'm taking you to the dentist, and that is final."

Antigua led Bun toward the office that Dr. Brushy shared with his twin sister, Doc Fixit.

"Why are you being so mean?" Bun said.

"I am being your friend," Antigua replied. "A good friend would never let her best pal suffer."

"You don't want me to suffer, eh?" Bun scoffed. "I know what **nasty** things happen at the dentist!"

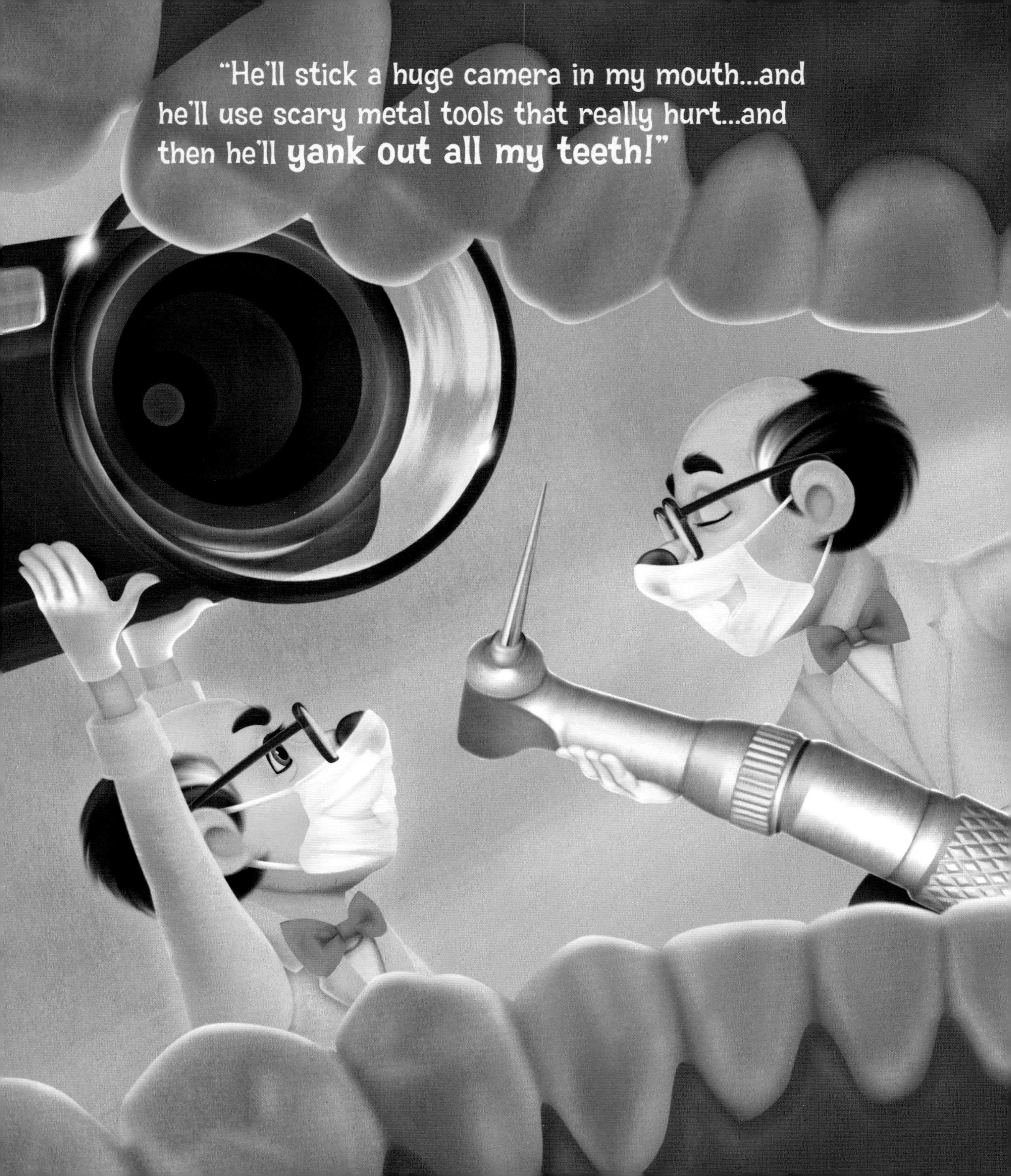

"He'll stick a huge camera in my mouth...and he'll use scary metal tools that really hurt...and then he'll **yank out all my teeth!**"

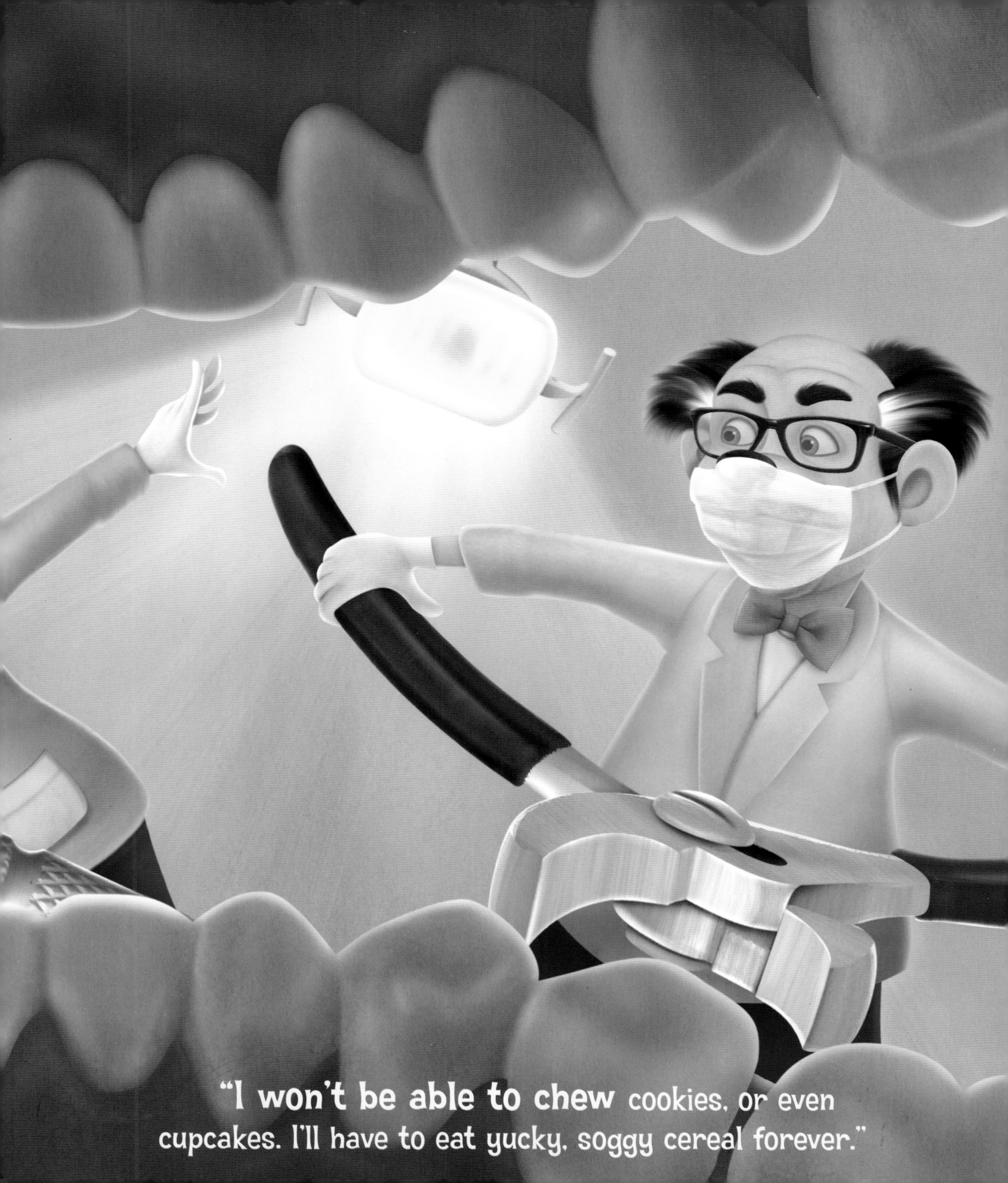

"I won't be able to chew cookies, or even cupcakes. I'll have to eat yucky, soggy cereal forever."

Antigua and Bun reached the door to Dr. Brushy's office. "I've seen Dr. Brushy many times," Antigua said. "He'll take great care of your smile."

"Fine," Bun huffed. "But when Dr. Brushy steals all my teeth, you'll have to feed me."

Antigua entered the office with Bun. Dr. Brushy greeted them with a friendly wave. "Antigua, my dear!" Dr. Brushy said.

"Hi, Dr. Brushy!" Antigua said. "Bun has a toothache. **Can you help him?"**

Bun joined Brushy in the exam room. "Before we start, Bun, I need you to put on this special vest," Brushy said. "Be careful; it's a little heavy."

"This looks sort of like an apron I'd wear in my bakery," Bun said.

"Please sit very still," Brushy said. "The machine next to you will make some funny noises, but it won't hurt you." Bun did what Brushy said. Brushy flipped a switch, and the machine began to hum and click for a few seconds.

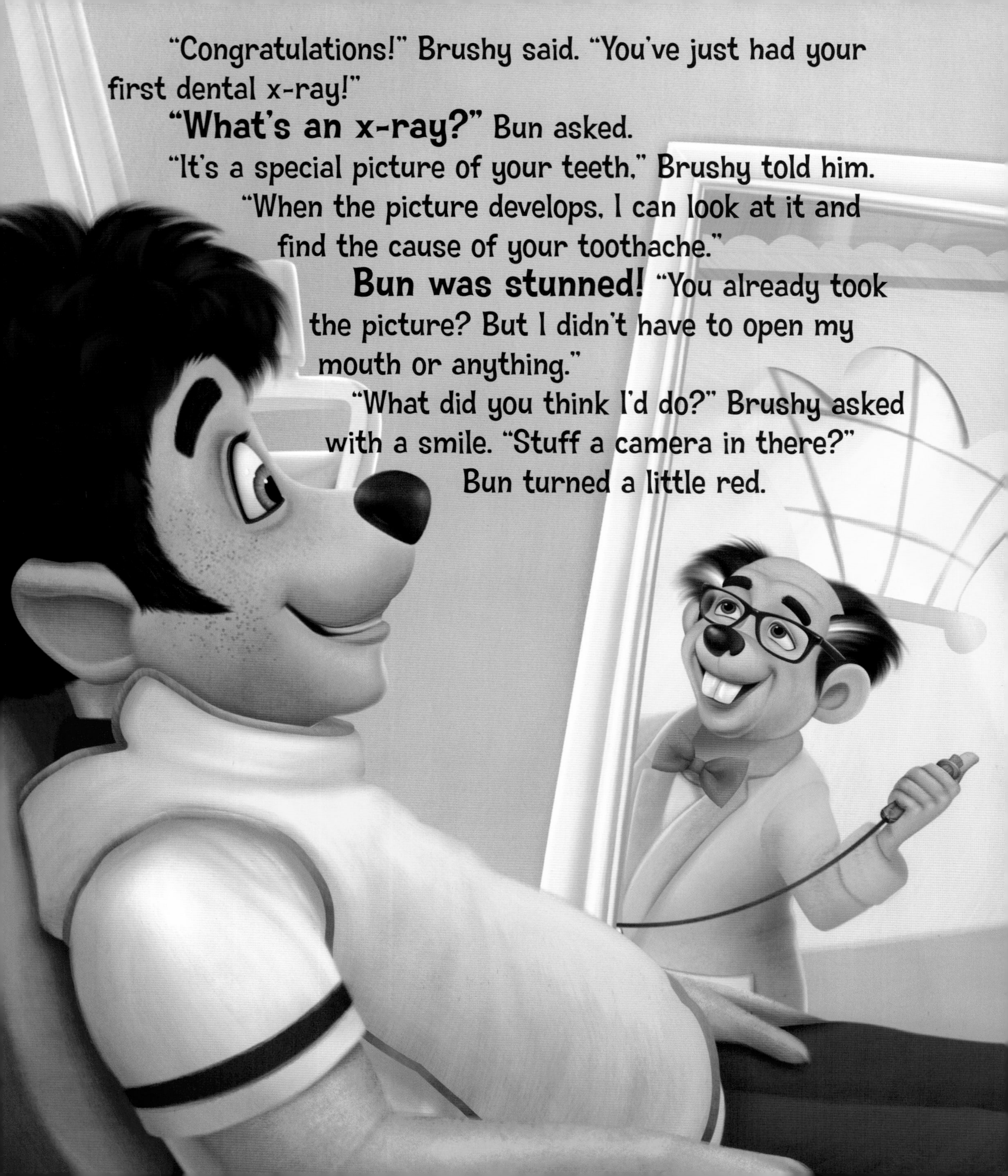

"Congratulations!" Brushy said. "You've just had your first dental x-ray!"

"What's an x-ray?" Bun asked.

"It's a special picture of your teeth," Brushy told him. "When the picture develops, I can look at it and find the cause of your toothache."

Bun was stunned! "You already took the picture? But I didn't have to open my mouth or anything."

"What did you think I'd do?" Brushy asked with a smile. "Stuff a camera in there?"

Bun turned a little red.

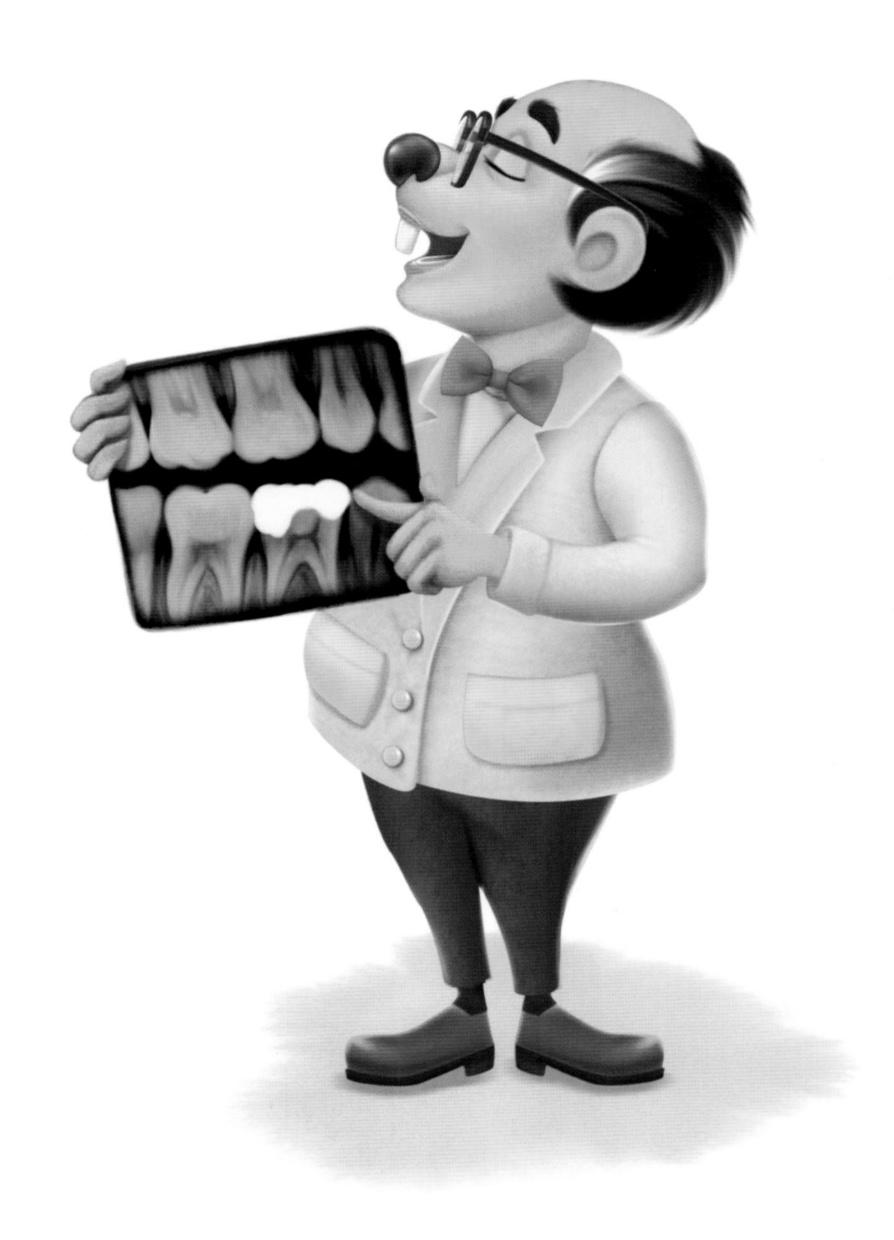

Soon, Bun's x-ray was ready. "I think I see the trouble, Bun," Brushy said. "Do you see that white spot on your tooth? **That, my friend, is a cavity."**

"A cavity! That's horrible!" Bun howled. "Right?"

"Well, a cavity is not good news," Brushy began. "But it is a very common problem. A cavity is a weak spot or hole on the outside of your tooth. Luckily, I know just how to deal with it."

"I knew it," Bun sighed. "You're going to yank out my teeth. **Goodbye, crispy cookies; hello, mushy cereal.**"

"Oh, no, I won't have to pull out any of your teeth," Brushy said. "That does happen sometimes, but only in real emergencies. Dentists always do their best to help your teeth so they do not have to be removed. All we need to do is clean out the cavity."

"Will that hurt?" Bun asked nervously.

"I'll be honest," Brushy said. "You might feel a little pain while I am working. But I will give you medicine before we start to help prevent that. And when I am done, I promise, you'll feel a hundred times better than you do now."

Bun decided to trust Dr. Brushy. Before they got to work, Brushy showed Bun all of his tools. That way, Bun would not be scared or surprised. **"I'm ready,"** Bun said.

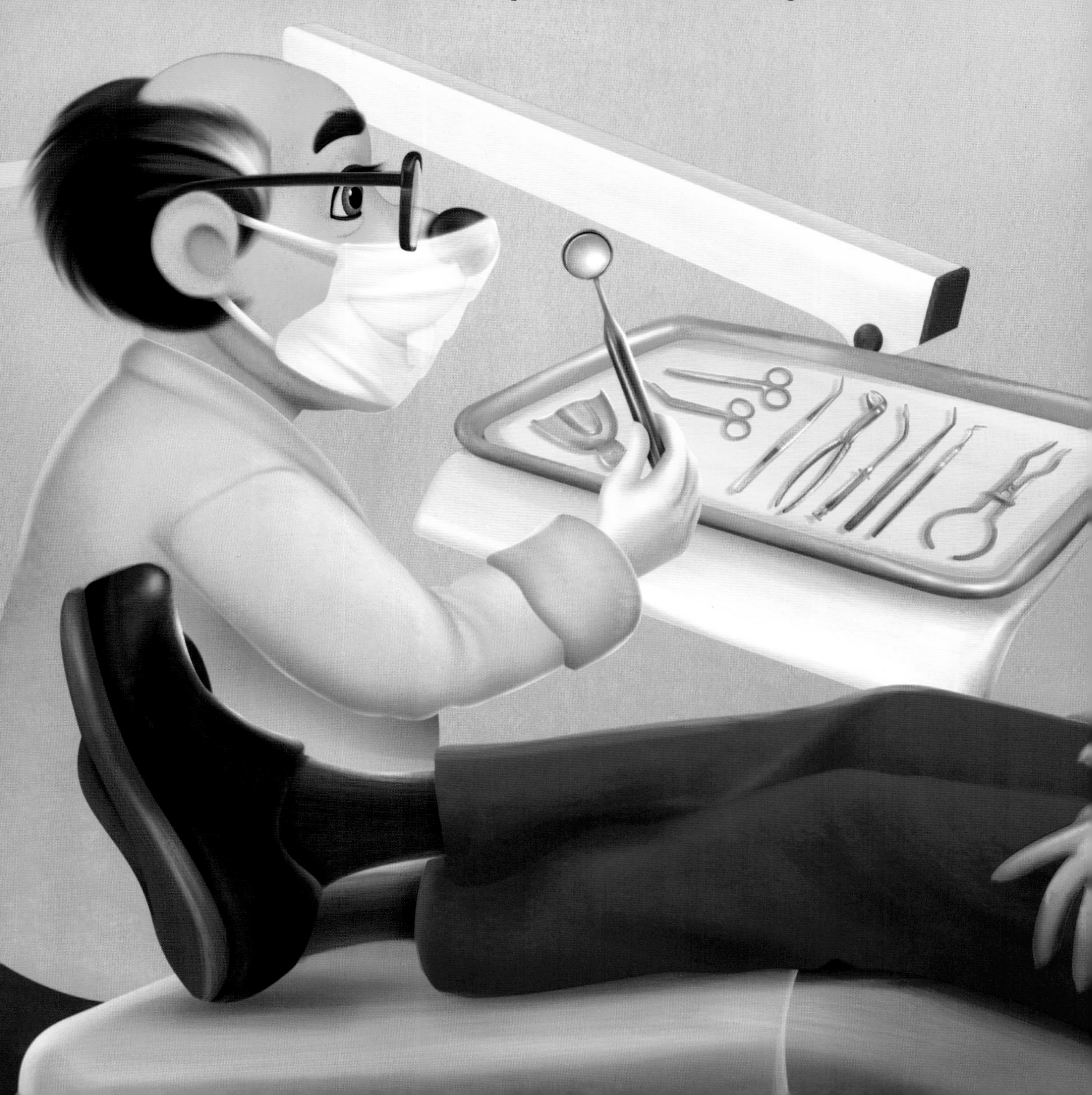

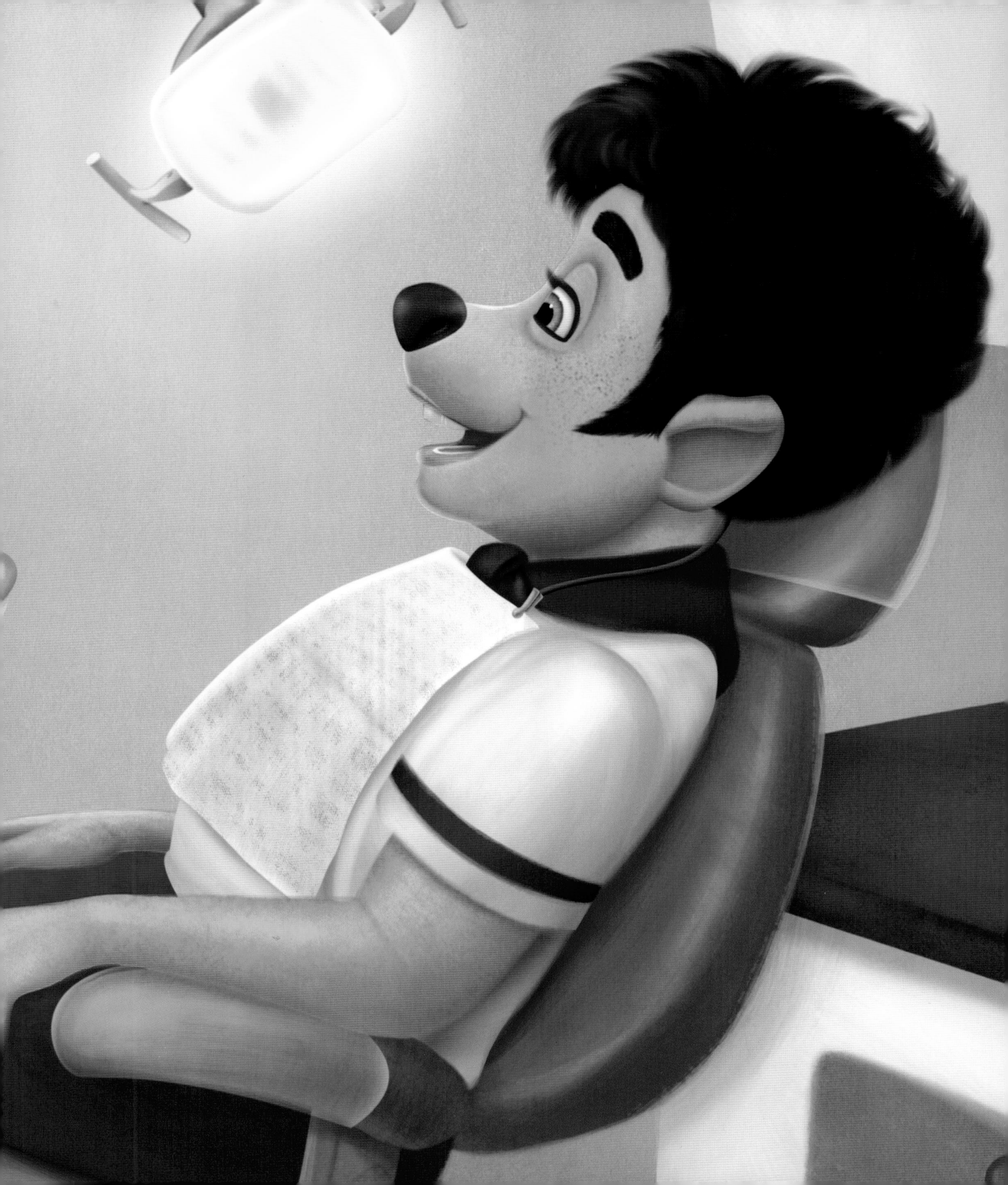

Before long, Bun was good as new. "I feel so much better!" he told Antigua in the waiting room. "I should have listened to you all along. **Thanks for being such a good friend."**

"You took great care of me, Dr. Brushy...but I don't want any more cavities," Bun said. "How can I keep them away?"

"One key to a healthy smile is to **brush** your teeth and **floss** twice every day," Brushy said.

"There's also something else," Brushy added. "I know you have a sweet tooth, Bun. But the germs that cause cavities love sugar. If you cut back on sugar, that can help fight cavities."

"No more sweets?" Bun said. "Antigua, this guy is bananas!"

"I didn't say 'no more sweets,'" Brushy said. "Even I like a piece of pie now and then. But, it is not good for your teeth to eat cupcakes and cookies all day long. Perhaps you could try something new."

Brushy pointed to a plate on the table. "Have a fresh carrot stick. I keep a special stash in case I get hungry at work."

Bun held up the carrot and smirked. "There's no frosting or anything," he said. But then he took a bite... and his eyes grew wide. **"Holy plum pudding!"** Bun said. "It's crunchy and juicy, and it's a little sweet, too!"

"You see?" Brushy said. "Lots of healthful foods taste great—without dumping sugar all over them."

Back at the bakery, Bun began to experiment with new, more healthful foods. Soon, he wasn't famous for just his sweets. Midlandians loved his salads, his toasted apple slices, and even his peanut butter crackers! Bun still ate cookies sometimes, but he was happy to have so many more choices. And as he told his customers, "**My teeth are a lot happier, too!**"

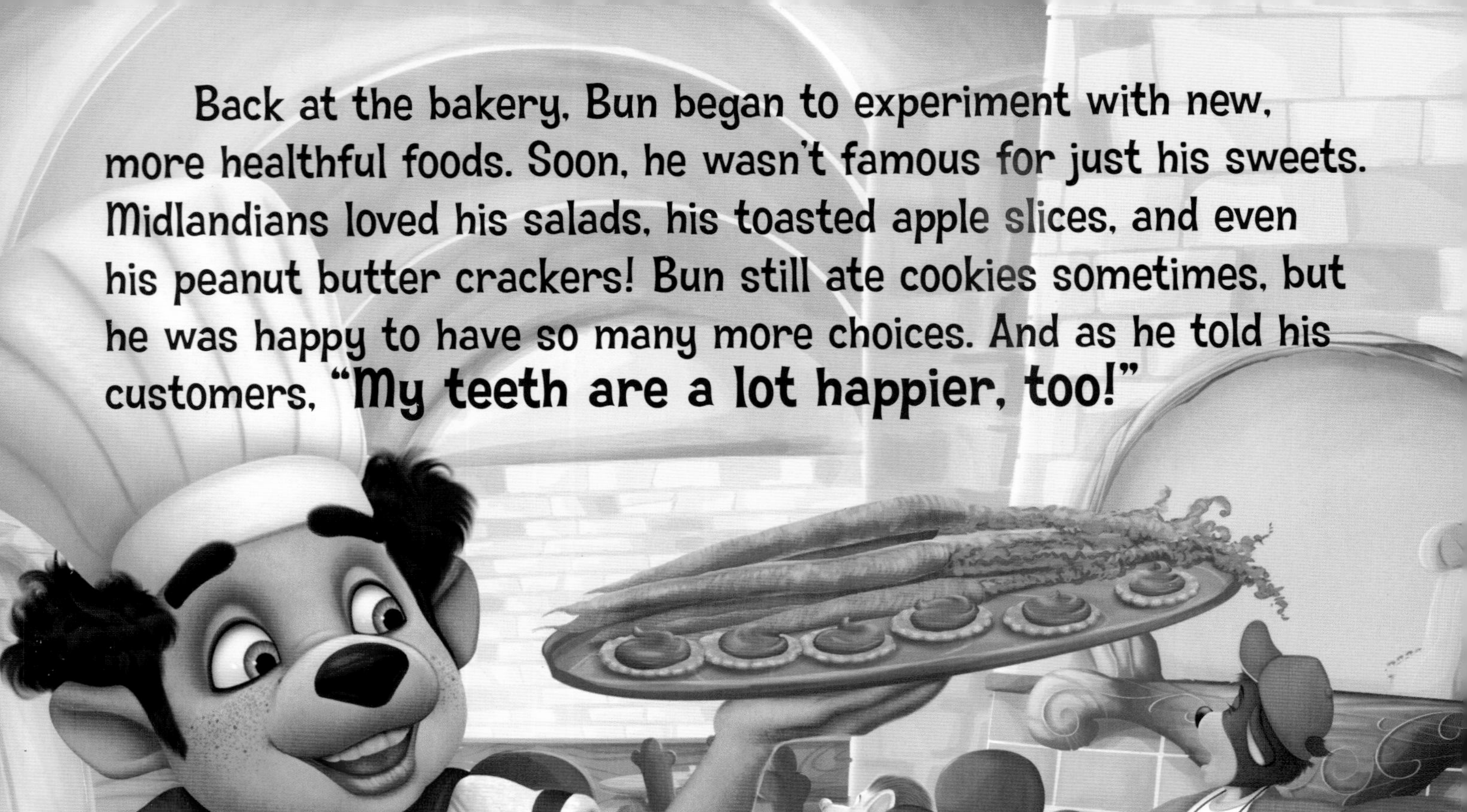

Discussion Questions

Have you ever been to the dentist?
Why did you go?
How was your visit?

Pretend that you have a friend who is afraid of going to the dentist. How would you help your friend?